malkin child

malkin child

Livi Michael

foxtail

First published in hardback in 2012 by Foxtail,
an imprint of Litfest Publications.
This paperback edition published in 2012.

Litfest
The Storey
Meeting House Lane
Lancaster LA1 1TH
Company Registered in England and Wales no. 1494221
Registered Charity no. 510670

ISBN 978-0-9540880-3-3

FSC

Cover design by Morph Films
Litfest wish to thank Lancaster City Council and Lancashire County Council.

This book is dedicated to Sandy Williams,
who made a difference.

A long time ago, in the Forest of Pendle, there lived a family.

There was a grandmother, who was known as Old Demdike, a mother, Elizabeth or Lizzie Device, and three children, Alizon, James and Jennet.

Jennet was the youngest member of this family, about nine years old when this story begins.

Not *this* story – it's *my* story!

She was several years younger than Alizon or James, and she always felt that she was different from the others.

I *am* different! That's because I've got a different father.

7

This family all lived together in a house called Malkin Tower, at the foot of Pendle Hill.

You're telling it all wrong! It's *my* family, and Malkin Tower was *my* house. And this is *my* story! You can't tell it, because it's *mine!*

Well –

Mine!

Can't I just –

No. I'm going to tell my story, about my family, and where we lived, and what happened to us there.

Malkin Tower

Our House

First off, it wasn't really a tower – more of a tumbledown cottage with one room and a leaking roof. There was a bare dirt floor and no windows apart from two slits close to the roof. The walls were black with smoke because we had to keep the fire going, to brew up the broth and to keep Our Granny's old bones warm.

That's her own bones, of course, and the ones she kept in a bag and shook from time to time to keep them lively.

In winter, whenever the door opened, the fire'd go out, and Our Granny'd yell, 'My old bones are freezing!' and we'd have to start lighting the fire all over again.

Course, the door was always opening and shutting. We had to go in and out. And sometimes the wind would bang it nearly off its hinges.

And other times, it would open and shut all on its own, but I'll tell you about that later.

The point is, our house was hot and smoky in summer, when you might want it cool, and cold and leaky in winter, when all you want is a bit of warm.

And it was my job to gather enough wood to keep the fire going. Which you'd think would've been easy, with us living in a forest. But the Forest of Pendle wasn't really a forest, just like Malkin Tower wasn't a tower.

For a start there weren't any trees – or not many. There was marshland and pasture for cows and sheep, but only a few clumps of woodland, apart from Trawden Wood. So I had to search far and wide for sticks.

When I asked Our Granny why it was called a forest when there weren't any trees, she said it was for the same reason as the house was called Malkin Tower – so folk wouldn't know what to look for. But Our Ma said it was because it was a hunting ground for the king.

Yes – there was a king of Pendle Forest! And this was his hunting ground – where he kept his deer and wild boar. I never saw him though, and I didn't see many deer or wild boar either. But I could see…

ur Hill

It'd be hard not to see it, because it's the biggest thing there is. The top of it's so high it's covered in mist. When you're at the top you can see the whole world!

It was the first thing we saw when we got up, and the last thing we saw when we went to bed.

First thing Granny did when she woke up was sniff it. She was nearly blind, Our Granny, but she could sniff out more than other folk could see. Like when a cut was going bad, or when trouble was coming, and when weather was on the way. Every morning she stood at the doorway and sniffed and said,

Pendle Hill, Pendle Hill,
Is thy shadow warm or chill,
Bring you fair or foul?

Mainly it brought us rain. But Granny could even tell us what sort.

Mizzlin' forenoon, hossin' after, or, *sylin' all day long.*

Even when the sun shone Our Hill cast its great shadow over

us. That's because we lived on the wrong side of it. Other folk lived on other sides of it, of course, but we didn't have anything to do with them. The hill kept us all in place.

Our Granny always said that nothing good came from the other side of Pendle Hill, and James always said that's why my dad came from there. I said, how come James was from this side then?

James was just jealous, because his and Alizon's dad died before I was born, and then a man came from over Our Hill, who turned out to be…

My Dad

I've never seen him, just like I've never seen the king.

That made me think he might *be* the king!

James said he was a no-good drifter, but what would he know?

I bet he went hunting, like kings do. He was probably looking for me, only he couldn't find the way back.

James said as soon as he saw me he'd run the other way.

But I always thought he'd come back for me, on a big

14

white horse, or in a shiny carriage. That'd show James!

I used to ask Our Ma about him, but she said I'd wear her into the ground, asking questions. And then she'd send me out, looking for sticks. It wasn't easy getting answers out of…

Our Ma

If I said, *where are you going, Ma?* She'd say, *following road,* or, *up hill and down dale.* And if I asked when she'd be back, she'd say, *haven't you swept that floor yet?* So it was always best not to ask.

She wore a cloth wrapped round her head and pulled down a bit so no one could see her face full on. That was because she never liked folk looking at her eye. They said that the devil looked out of it, and if she turned it on you something bad would happen – you'd fall sick or come out in blotches like Blaize Hargrieves.

Truth was, Our Granny dropped her on her head when she was little, and she was never the same after. One eye looked a bit bigger than the other, and it didn't move the same.

It was true, though, that if she looked at you with

it, you had to watch out. It's like she knew what you were thinking.

She went out every day, Our Ma, with her sleeves rolled up and her hair scraped back, looking for work. Knocking on doors, offering to milk the cow or card some wool, all for a penny here, or a jug of milk there. *Works herself to the bone,* Our Granny'd say and she'd rattle her bag of bones at her.

There was nothing Our Ma couldn't do. She'd climb up on the roof to fix it, or saw wood to mend the door. And she always brought something home for…

Granny's Pot

It hung over the fire, which kept it bubbling, and from time to time Granny'd throw something in and give it a good stir. We were all supposed to bring something home to be thrown in, even if it was only a beetle.

It was best not to ask what was for tea.

Generally, if I did ask, Granny'd say, *gizzards,* or, *gruel.*

Now, I know what gruel is – I've been eating it my whole life – but I've never found out what a gizzard is.

I can tell you what they look like, though. Greyish. Lumpy. And chewy.

Not everything Granny cooked was food. People paid her to cook things up for them. Like potions. Some of the really smelly brews were potions. Like when James fell out of a tree, looking for eggs, and hurt his arm, Granny brewed up a potion that stank our house out for days. And she stood over it, muttering,

> *Like bone strain, so blood stain, so joint sprain,*
> *Bone to bone, blood to blood, joint to joint,*
> *So they be glued.*

And do you know, the very next morning his arm was right as rain!

Mind you, she tried the same thing on Christopher Nutter's mother's arthritis, and he came round saying she'd grown a hump.

We got a lot of complaints like that.

Ma always said it was best not to let people in. James said it would've been best if she'd not let my dad in. I never liked…

Our James

Once, when I said I was hungry, he made me eat a worm. And he always made me clean up his mess, and he was always showing off. He said he had magical powers. I said, how come he was so ugly then?

When I was small, he said he could show me a real goblin, but it was so horrible I might wet myself with fright.

Course, I said I wouldn't, and I begged him to show me, so he made me look down the well, and all I could see was me in the water. And when I said there wasn't any goblin, he pushed me in, and said he'd told me I'd wet myself!

He'd get in trouble for these things, of course, but not as much trouble as I'd have liked. That's because Our Ma was soft on him. Especially once he was big, and he could be the one to climb on the roof or fix the door.

He'd go out poaching and bring back things for Granny's pot, like a squirrel, or a rabbit, or bird that had fallen. Even when he did a day's work he'd get into trouble for being drunk or nicking things. Lots of people complained about James, but Our Ma wouldn't let them in. Her bad eye went soft when she looked at him. *He's the man of the house,* she'd say.

But I couldn't see that we needed a man of the house

when we'd got Our Ma, and Our Granny, and…

Our Alizon

She was the eldest, and I was the youngest, but we had to share a bed. Her feet were always cold, and she used me to warm them up on. Then she'd start snoring and I'd be left wide awake and freezing!

Her main job was to go out begging. She never liked it, though. She said it made her feel poorly.

Ooh, Our Ma, I'm feeling right poorly, she used to say. But Ma wouldn't have it. *Get your shawl on, girl, and get on road. Fresh air'll do you good.*

She took me out with her, when I was small, because she said it was useful having a littl'un with her.

Lady, spare a penny for my little sister, who's sick, or, *can you spare us a cup of milk, my little sister's failing fast.*

And I'd stand there looking sorry for myself. Which wasn't hard when I'd been out all day in the cold and wet.

Folk who wouldn't usually stop would give us a penny, or something to eat, *for the babby.* I've always been small for my size and some folk thought I was a babby till I was six or seven.

But then I grew a bit and I wasn't so useful any more.

I didn't mind being left behind. There was nothing worse than having to knock on doors that wouldn't open, or waiting on lonely roads until someone came by. Sometimes no one came by for hundreds of hours, especially when the weather was bad.

Weather was always bad. And some people'd open their doors at first, then shut them quickly when they saw us.

Nowt so cold as charity, Our Granny always said.

Anyway, I got a different job, gathering sticks for Granny's fire. And there was no end to that, for Granny's bones were always cold. And she'd always got something brewing and smelling the house out in that old pot of hers.

But sometimes I'd still arrange to meet Our Alizon. You see, the best place for gathering sticks was Trawden Wood, and I didn't like being there on my own, not when the light was fading. Everyone knew there were goblins in Trawden Wood. And wolves, maybe, and other things no one had a name for that lived in holes and crawled about in the darkness. Alizon didn't like it either – she was scared of her own shadow, Our Alizon. So we'd arrange to meet up and go through it together, as fast as we could. But that didn't stop…

The Scariest Thing that Ever Happened to Me and Our Alizon in Trawden Wood

It was later than we thought when we met up, and the trees were up to their usual stuff, murmuring and whispering to one another in the darkness. And if you got too close they'd touch your shoulders with their long, twiggy fingers. So me and Our Alizon stayed close to one another, holding hands, not speaking, in case anything was listening.

Soon as we got in, all the rest of the light drained off. Nothing was quite what it seemed. For instance, I nearly bumped into a hairy old man, and I was about to yell, when I saw it was only a tree stump covered with ivy.

All the trees had holes in their trunks, like open mouths.

We could hear the drip, drip, drip of rain on leaves, and it sounded a bit like footsteps.

Pad, pad, pad.

Not human footsteps.

Alizon looked round fearfully and I shifted my bundle of sticks under my arm and prepared to run. Something rustled through the bushes, first one side, then the other.

We moved away from where we thought the noise was, but it moved with us.

Pad, pad, pad, pad.

And behind us.

Rustle, rustle, rustle.

Then the whistling started.

It was like no whistling I'd ever heard before – a high-pitched, lonely sound that seemed like it was hundreds of miles away, and at the same time right in front of us. Or just behind. Or to the left.

Just when we thought we'd worked out where it was coming from, another whistle joined it, coming at us from a different place. And then another.

My grip tightened on Alizon's hand. 'What is it?' I whispered, but she only shook her head, and her eyes were very bright.

When a fourth whistle started we didn't say anything else – we ran. Stumbling and blundering in the one direction there was no whistling from.

Trawden Wood's not that big, but it seemed like we were being driven round and round it – until we dropped dead from running, or went mad with fright.

Then, at last, the trees started to clear. Soon there were only two or three left, then one, and then we were on the road again, panting and quivering with fright.

'What – was – *that?*' I managed to say.

Our Alizon could hardly speak either, but she said, 'Dogs.'

Dogs?

Whistling dogs?

I couldn't ask her, because she'd set off sharpish, keen to get home before it got any darker. I trotted after her saying, 'I didn't know dogs could whistle.'

'Tibb can,' she said. And suddenly everything was clear. It won't be clear to you, because I haven't told you about Tibb yet, or the rest of them. I've told you about Our Granny, and Our Ma, Our Alizon and Our James, but not about…

Our Demons

There were four of them, Dandy, Ball and Tibb. And Our Alizon's, that she wouldn't name. Our Granny said she'd have to, because a demon doesn't have full power till you give it a name.

Our Alizon said her demon had more than enough power already, and she was too feared to give it a name.

I wouldn't have been scared if I'd had a demon. I'd have called it Blackjack, and it would've gone everywhere with me, and answered my call.

But I didn't have one. I couldn't even see them.

James said I'd never have one, and the reason was, I had a different father.

But Granny said I'd have one when the time came. And I'd know when that was because I'd start seeing them. Then I'd have to bring one into my power.

Not that this lot seemed to be in anyone's power. They just seemed to do what they liked.

Three of them were in the shape of hounds, one black – that's Dandy, James's demon; one brown – that's Ball, Our Ma's demon. Alizon's, that had no name, was either spotted or black, so I was told. And one of them was half black and half brown. That was Tibb, Granny's demon. He could take the shape of a human man, or boy, as well as a dog. He was master of them all.

Master of the Whistling Dogs.

He was definitely the most trouble – the others all barked to his whistle. But between them those demons caused havoc in Our House. Milk spilt, pot tipped over or someone tripped up – you knew the demons were up to their old tricks again. Doors'd bang and the fire'd go out and wouldn't light again, broth spilt and more of the roof fell in. Alizon'd come home with nothing but a set of broken eggs, and James'd come back drunk.

Once, James stole some bacon, and it kept disappearing, and Our Ma accused Granny of eating it, but Granny said the demons took it – and her with bacon fat all over her chin!

Other times, when James came back with nowt, he'd say that Dandy had run off with his stuff.

He was always threatening to set Dandy on me if I didn't do as he said.

I wished I had a demon – bigger and scarier than James's! He'd look like Dandy, but with horns. He'd do more tricks and see James off.

But I didn't have a demon. Same as I couldn't do spells.

I wished and wished for more food, or for a house that didn't leak. I tried to put a curse on James, so that the goblins'd get him, or he'd grow boils on his bum, but nothing happened. He'd just laugh at me and say I didn't have the power and I never would have. And I'd never have a demon, because I couldn't even see one.

That night, though, when we ran through Trawden Wood – that was the first time I *thought* I could see them. I was sure I could see dark shapes flitting past as we ran. I was too scared to look properly, and when I did, they disappeared.

Then, when we got into Our House, there was Our Granny, stirring the pot as usual, over the flames. She cackled when she saw our faces. 'Thought you needed chivvying on a bit,' she said.

There was a lot I could've said to that, but I didn't say anything, because, for the first time ever, I could see the shadow of something hovering round her, waiting for a feed. A small man, in a big hat.

I didn't say anything because I wasn't sure. But I glared at him as I went past, and I was sure I could see him glaring back.

Or was he grinning?

I stood by Alizon, while she took off her wet shawl, but I kept my eye on him all the time.

Then Ma came in with James, and lit the rush lights, and we all had some stew, which wasn't quite as evil as it smelled, and then we sat round the fire, playing knucklebones with Granny's teeth.

She got them from a graveyard. She said she used them to cure toothache, but we all used them like dice.

Times like this, we forgot about the cold, and the storm outside, because we were inside, around a fire, all of us. Humans and demons. That night, I could see three shadow hounds sitting round and panting in the flames, and Tibb with his feet up, sitting on nothing much at all.

I looked and looked, but I couldn't see my demon yet. And soon I felt sleepy, and started yawning fit to split my head. I had to go and lie down on our bed in the corner of the room. I went on watching Tibb, though, and I had the feeling that he was watching back. Before I fell asleep I muttered at him, 'You ain't half naughty, Tibb,' and for the first time ever I could hear him, clear as day.

'Well, I'm a demon, en't I?' he said.

And there was nothing I could say to that.

But other folk had plenty to say:

Demdike lives with Demdike's brood,
Cooking up the devil's food,
Alizon, James, and Skinny Jen,
Squinting Lizzie with her eyes that sken,
Cooking up trouble in the devil's hour,
In that crooked house called Malkin Tower.

That's what folk said when they thought we weren't listening. They said Our House was the devil's house, but what I want to know is, if it *was* his house, why didn't he fix it? He didn't fix our roof, or light the fire when it went out. He didn't make us rich. If James hadn't stolen food from time to time, we'd just go hungry.

But the cursing – well that seemed to work, some of the time. But nothing good ever came of that. That was the start of all the trouble.

Trouble

The Pedlar

Winter was nearly over, but spring hadn't happened yet, and as everyone knows, bad stuff happens in winter. Like, there was no work for Our Ma and no food for Our James to poach, and no one on the roads for Our Alizon to beg from. Our Granny's old bones played up, and I had to go out in all weathers looking for sticks until my fingers turned blue.

But we were almost through this winter, and it could have been a lot worse, and March had come so it was nearly spring.

On a grey day when the wind was up with a touch of rain in it to keep it sharp, Our Alizon set off begging with just a thin shawl round her shoulders.

I had to stay in and help Granny because she could hardly move. It was a long day, but before the last of the light had disappeared, Our Alizon came back.

I could hear her talking to Our Ma, in a high-pitched kind of way. Ma just grunted, then said, 'Get inside. We'll bolt the door.'

Both my ears pricked up at that. We never bolted the door, since there was nothing to rob.

Alizon came in with her eyes as big as saucepans and her lips pressed together. When I said, 'What's up?' she only gave a little shake of her head.

She sat shivering by the fire, and after a moment I saw the shadow of a big dog cross the room to sit at her feet.

Then Our Ma came in, looking grim, and bolted the door.

'Why are you doing that, Ma?' I asked, but she only said, 'Never you mind.'

I did mind, though.

We all went to bed without talking, and as soon as Our Alizon lay down I started kicking her shins with my bare feet.

'Stop it,' she said, moving her legs around.

'Tell me what's happened, then,' I said, and she moved her legs some more. But I was good at this, I could keep it up all night if I had to.

I nearly had to! It took a lot to get it out of her because she was really, really scared. But in the end she told me, looking one way and then another as if something bad might be listening, and speaking so low I could hardly hear.

She told me she'd been out all day and had no luck begging – there was hardly anyone on the roads, and the people in houses kept their doors locked against the wind.

Then she saw the pedlar.

He was well known in these parts. He walked all

day long, over the hills – not just Our Hill, but all of them, carrying a bundle of goods for sale.

He sold pots and pans, rope and thread, pegs and pins. And little story books with pictures of goblins and giants in them and kings in castles, wearing crowns! He sold dolls and toy soldiers made from pegs. And even a magic lantern! I never got to see it, though. Even if he called by Our House – which he hardly ever did, he could see we had no money – Our Ma always sent him packing.

I wanted her to let him untie his bundle so I could look through it first, and *then* send him packing! But she never did. I only knew what he sold because I'd heard folk talking about it.

Anyway, Our Alizon saw this pedlar on the road. She'd had no luck that day, and she was desperate to get home, but Our Ma always said, *never come back to your own door empty-handed,* so she started following him. Asking him for the least thing from his bundle – a packet of pins.

That was her first mistake.

For starters, she'd have done better to ask for something bigger that cost more. Because with the weather being so cold and dampish, the pedlar told her he wouldn't untie his bundle just to look for one packet of pins.

'*Please,* sir,' Our Alizon said, 'just one little packet.'

Now, of course she didn't say she'd got no money and couldn't pay, but maybe the pedlar knew, for he wouldn't untie his bundle. And when she wouldn't leave him alone, he called her a bad name.

'What?' I asked. 'What did he call you?'

But she wouldn't tell me. She said it was too bad.

And that's when she made her second mistake.

She cursed him with her most fearful curse!

Course, she wouldn't tell me what it was. But it must've been a good one, because he looked at her and tried to speak but couldn't, then his eyes rolled back and he fell to the ground and lay there as though he was dead!

I wish I'd been there!

All the times I'd tried to put a curse on James and nothing happened!

Our Alizon didn't know what to do. She ran up to the pedlar and called to him and tried to get him to sit up or speak, but he couldn't do either.

Then, in the distance, she saw two men travelling towards her on that same road, so she ran and hid herself quick, in a copse of trees.

She watched while they came up to the pedlar, and knelt over him, then managed to pick him up between them.

Then, and this was her third mistake, she followed

them a little way, just to see that he was all right.

When I say mistake, I mean one of them must've seen her – either that or the pedlar got suddenly better, because one way or another they found out who she was.

A Stranger Comes to Our House

Days passed and nothing happened. Nothing usually happened, but now it was as though we were all waiting, though nobody'd tell me what for. No one said anything, apart from Our Granny, who sat by the fire, chewing and saying, *No cloud without rain,* or, *crows fly to land, storm's at hand,* and cheery stuff like that.

Then one day we were all sitting round our fire, eating gruel, and the next thing we knew there was a terrific banging on our door.

James leapt up, but Our Ma told him to sit down again. She'd not open the door, Our Ma, just because someone was banging it off its hinges.

Next thing we heard was a big voice, deep and rough edged.

'My name is Abraham Law,' it said. 'Son of the pedlar, John Law.'

Alizon looked at Our Ma with her big eyes, and started to speak, but Ma hushed her harshly. Then she went up to the door, but she didn't open it. She said, 'What do you want?'

'I've come for Alizon Device,' said the voice. Our James squared up at once, but Our Ma said, 'You've come, and you can go again.'

'Who am I speaking to?' said the voice.

Like Ma'd tell him. Granny cackled suddenly. 'The wind,' she said. 'He's talking to the wind!'

No one took any notice. Then the voice spoke slow and heavy.

'I've come about my father,' it said. 'He's lying in Colne speechless, with the left side lamed all save one eye.'

Alizon was listening with her hand pressed to her mouth, but as the stranger started knocking again, she ran forward crying, 'It's all right, Ma, let him in!'

'Aye, let him,' said James, ready for a fight.

Our Ma looked at them both, then suddenly flung the door open and glared at the stranger with the full force of her bad eye.

'Well,' she said. 'If your father's lying sick in Colne, what are you doing here?'

But the stranger, who was broad and square-shaped

in his woollen clothes, wasn't put off that easy. He looked past Our Ma to where Alizon was hovering behind, and said, 'Are you Alizon Device?'

'I am,' quavered Alizon.

'Will you come with me?' he said, and slowly, fearfully, Alizon nodded, even as Our Ma said, 'Nay, she'll not.'

'I mean you no harm,' said the stranger, still talking to Alizon, not Our Ma. 'I'm hoping you can mend what you've done.'

'She's done nothing,' said Ma, but at the same time, Alizon said, 'It's all right, Ma – let me – I want to go.'

Our Ma looked grimmer than ever, but Alizon wrapped herself in her shawl and stepped outside to the stranger. And they went off together, leaving Our House suddenly empty and cold.

And you could say that that was her fourth mistake, going off like that. Because that's when all the bad stuff happened.

Bad Stuff

When things go wrong, you can't help thinking that they could've turned out different. Our Ma could've closed the door in the stranger's face, told him that none of us knew what he was talking about. Or she could've said, *there's no one here by the name of Alizon Device,* and we'd all have backed her up. And Our Alizon needn't have gone with him – she could have said she'd never seen the pedlar, let alone cursed him. Then it would've been the pedlar's word against Our Alizon's.

I said as much to her when she got back that night, looking right sorry for herself. But she said she couldn't have done that, not with him lying there so poorly. She had to try to make him better.

And then she burst into tears.

See – soft as butter, Our Alizon!

She told us she'd tried to undo the spell she'd put on him, and she'd tried out another spell for healing – in front of everyone at the inn!

Course, none of it worked. All she did was prove to everyone she's a witch.

Our Ma groaned aloud and James said she'd got less sense than a headless hen. But Alizon said, 'They knew anyway.'

'How?' I asked her. 'How did they know?'

'Because – the pedlar said he saw something,' she said, looking fearfully at Our Ma. 'A demon – like a big dog – at the very moment I cursed him!'

Well! I thought. All the times I'd tried to see a demon and couldn't!

'How come he could see it?' I asked, but everyone shut me up. Because Our Alizon said that the pedlar's son was going to report her to the JP.

'What's a JP?' I asked, but of course no one'd tell me that either. And when I kept asking questions, I was told to get into bed.

Our Alizon got in after, and I could feel how cold she was; not just her feet, she was chilled right through and shaking. I tucked myself into her and whispered, 'Don't fret, Alizon – it'll be all right.'

'No it won't,' she said. And she was right.

More Bad Stuff

After that, things started happening fast. Two Officers of the Law came, in their funny hats. I knew what they were because

James had been in trouble before. They rapped on our door even though it was open, and Our Ma said, 'Who's there?' even though she could see.

There was a tall thin one and a short fat one, and the short fat one said, 'We've come for the young maid, Alizon Device.'

'She's not here,' said James, just as Alizon stepped forward, and Our Ma said, 'What do you want with her?'

'She's to be taken before the Justice of the Peace.'

I opened my mouth to ask what that was, but he said, 'That's Master Roger Nowell, of Read Hall.'

None of us knew that name, so the thin one said, 'Him that was High Sheriff of all Lancashire – do you know nothing in these parts?'

At this James got very rude – I can't even tell you what he said, but one of the Officers lunged at him and Our Ma leapt between them, defending James as usual, and the end of it was they were all bundled into a cart!

Me and Our Granny stood staring after them as they were driven away.

I looked at Granny, but she just shuffled back into the house.

'Can't you do a spell?' I said, following her, but she only said, 'My old bones are cold.' And she huddled up to the fire clutching them.

'You could curse them, Granny,' I said. 'Make the wheels fall off that cart. Make them bring Ma and Alizon back!'

They could keep James.

But Granny just sat there, rocking herself, and crooning.

When Granny wouldn't answer me, I tried summoning Our Demons.

'Tibb,' I said in a low voice. 'Now's the time you might do something useful.' And, 'Come Dandy, come Ball.'

I looked and looked but there was no sign of them, not even the shadow of a tail.

I told you – that old witchcraft never works when you need it. Or at least, only the bad stuff ever works.

Hundreds of hours later, Our Ma and James came back – without Alizon.

'Where's Our Alizon, Ma? What've they done with her?' I asked. 'When's she coming home?'

No answer. But finally Ma said, 'She's not coming

home – they're keeping her. On suspicion of witchcraft.'

I thought everyone *knew* she was a witch!

'But why, Ma?' I wanted to know, and 'When will they set her free?' But all Ma would say was that she didn't know, and that this JP person was going to call our neighbours in for questioning.

Even Granny's face fell when she heard that. Our neighbours hated us!

Our Neighbours

Our main neighbours were the Whittles. They had a Granny, just like ours, and she was known as Chattox. Which I always thought was on account of her lips chattering away even when no one was listening.

She was hundreds of years old, was Chattox, and everyone was scared of her. Everyone knew she'd put a curse on Our Alizon's friend, Anne Nutter, who took sick and died. Our Ma always said she'd witched father to death.

That's James's and Alizon's father, not mine. He was so scared of Chattox he used to pay her a gift of oatmeal every year. And the year he didn't pay – he died!

My dad wouldn't have paid her. And he wouldn't have been scared either!

Now, at one time, Our Granny and Chattox were the best of friends. They would sit in Our House together for hundreds of hours, cackling by the fire. Then they had a falling out, but no one knew why.

Chattox always said she was the most powerful witch in these parts, but Granny said that *she* was, and maybe that was the start of it. But soon it was clear that Chattox hated Granny, and Granny hated Chattox, and folk round here didn't know who they were most scared of.

But anyway, the next time that old wagon came back, it carried both of them off. *For questioning,* was all the guards would say. But it'd be no use questioning Our Granny and Chattox – they'd just start blaming one another!

I couldn't understand any of this. Why had this Roger Nowell person kept Our Alizon and then taken Our Granny away?

When I asked James, he said it wasn't his fault, he hadn't said anything, but he looked so shifty I knew he was telling lies.

When I asked Our Ma, she just said, 'Scrape that pan.'

So I did scrape that pan, and sweep the yard, and I

gathered sticks as usual, and if I passed anyone, I tried to listen in on what they were saying. Rumours were flying, that more neighbours had been called in for questioning, and that this Roger Nowell would arrest everyone if he had to, until he got the information he needed.

No one'd talk to me, of course. Soon as they saw me, everyone'd stop talking.

But the next thing was that James's pal Billy's brother Robert said he'd seen them – Granny and Alizon, Chattox and Chattox's daughter Anne – being marched along the Old Road, under guard!

Our Granny, who can hardly stand up, never mind walk!

James's pal Billy's brother Robert ran along after them on the high path over the moor, until he worked out where they were going. To Lancaster, he said. Forty miles off!

'But why, Ma?' I asked, 'Why would they take them there?'

She didn't answer, she just looked kind of stunned. But James's pal Billy said, 'That's where the gaol is.'

I didn't even know what a gaol was, or where Lancaster was.

Apparently, it's in a castle.

The gaol, that is, not Lancaster.

I thought only kings lived in a castle!

Nothing like this had ever happened before – strangers coming in and taking our own folk away – and none of us knew what to do.

 *hat Our Ma Did*

'Do something, Ma,' I begged. 'Use your magic powers – make them help you!'

Well, she didn't, of course, because she couldn't. But maybe I put some kind of thought into her head, because the next thing I knew, she was holding a meeting, in Our House!

She wouldn't tell me anything about it, of course. Though it didn't stop me asking, 'What kind of meeting?'

'Never you mind.'

'Who's coming?'

'No one you know.'

'What will they eat?'

'Have you let that fire go out again?'

I had to ask, though, because there was never enough food to feed us, never mind other folk, coming to a *meeting*. And I soon found out the answer, because Our James stole a sheep.

A whole sheep! We had to build a special fire to roast it on.

You should've smelled it roasting. Mmmm! All that mutton!

Then folk started arriving. I'd never seen so many people in Our House! I didn't know who half of them were, but when I asked Our Ma, she just told me to stop mithering.

When I asked James, he said they were all witches, and they'd come from far and near – not just the other side of Our Hill. Some of them had come from a land called Yorkshire.

When I said I didn't believe him, he said Jennet Preston had come from Gisburn, in Yorkshire, and she'd flown all the way on a magic horse.

He must've thought I was daft!

Then he said there were twenty witches coming altogether, and I'd better stay out of the way in case they turned me into something nasty. Though not as nasty as I already was, he said.

Twenty witches in Malkin Tower! And they came just in time for dinner – they must've smelled the mutton.

'But why, Ma, why are they here?' I asked.

Our Ma said, 'Less talking and more work,' and, 'Stay

out of the way.'

So I did stay out of the way, though I kept watch. Some of them came with more food – one brought bacon, and another, beef, and yet another ale! Bacon, beef *and* mutton – I'd never had so much food on my plate! Then I sat in the pantry – or what we called the pantry – it was really just a dug-out space under the main room where we kept James's stolen food. It was big enough for me to hide myself in, though, and listen to what was said. And I could peep out.

There was lots of talk – about setting Our Alizon and Our Granny free, though no one knew how. Someone said they should name Our Alizon's demon, because that would grant her the power to set herself free. Then the woman called Jennet Preston, who James said came on a magic horse, from the land called Yorkshire, asked for help to get her own back on a man called Thomas Lister, who'd accused her of killing his father. She wanted everyone there to curse him, because, she said, 'Twenty witches are better than one.'

Soon everyone was drunk, and the talk got a bit wild. About blowing up the castle, and killing the gaoler and such. But by this time I'd eaten so much I started to feel sleepy, and my eyes began to close.

And then I saw them all differently. Wreathing in and amongst them were the shapes of animals: cats and hares, dogs and toads, horses and wolves.

Like smoke, kind of, but smoke with eyes.

Then when I woke up again, everyone was leaving. And I was wanted again, to help clear up the mess.

You've never seen such a mess! I don't know about twenty witches being better than one – they were definitely messier. That lot couldn't find their own mouths – never mind Lancaster gaol!

Granny's Teeth

Course, you can't have a meeting of twenty witches without folk knowing about it. Someone must've reported it to Roger Nowell, because the next thing was, those two Officers of the Law were back at Our House.

I came back from picking sticks in the wood for our fire, and there was the short fat one and the tall thin one again, with James.

Quick as lightning I nipped round the side of Our House, out of the way. I thought they'd come because James had stolen a sheep, but then I saw they were looking at something else.

I couldn't see what it was, but the short fat one said, 'Well – these are Very Serious Findings, Master Device. Very Serious Indeed.'

And James looked all red in the face. He wasn't full of swagger now – he looked like a dog that had been kicked.

'We'll be taking these to Read Hall,' said the thin one in his thin voice. Then James dropped something into a little pot, and I heard it rattle four times.

Suddenly I knew what it was. Teeth! It was Granny's teeth!

What did those men want with Granny's teeth?

Then I saw what else they'd got – a clay figure about as long as my arm and a bit cracked. I didn't know if it was a woman or a man. But I knew we were in trouble. Again.

As soon as they'd gone I came out of my hiding place.

'Who were they, James – who were those men you were talking to?'

'No one *you'd* know, Big-Ears!'

My ears might be big, but it's because I had to listen so hard – no one ever told me anything.

Next day, the big cart came back – only this time it was for me and Ma and James. We were all arrested!

Now I knew this wasn't good, of course, but I couldn't help feeling a bit excited about riding in a cart. It lurched and wobbled and we all rolled about from side to side. It took us to a big house on the other side of Our Hill. Our Ma glared like a demon the whole way, but all she said was, 'Say nothing, James, Jennet – do you hear me?' and we both had to promise that we wouldn't. I wouldn't dare say anything with Our Ma looking at me like that!

But when we got to the house we were all taken into separate rooms.

Separate rooms! I'd never been in a house with separate rooms before! And stairs!

I was taken into this big, square room with sun streaming in through the windows – we didn't even have windows at Malkin Tower – and everything was shiny – shiny wood and shiny glass. There was someone with his back to the window, but I couldn't hardly see him for all that shine.

But then the servant who took me in spoke his name. It was him…

Roger Nowell

There is just one truth, and it is mine;
How brightly can I make it shine?

Now I'd already promised Our Ma that I wouldn't say anything. What I didn't know was how hard that would be when someone kept asking questions.

I did the best I could.

He asked me if I knew there was a meeting, and if I had taken part, and I said, 'Yes sir,' and, 'no sir, not really sir'. Then he asked me if I had seen who was there and I said, 'Yes, there were about twenty people there and they were all witches.'

He seemed very pleased with this information – I had to repeat it twice. I began to wonder if he were a bit deaf.

Then I had to go out again and sit with Our Ma and she was looking all fierce. 'What did you tell him, child?' she said.

'Nothing, Ma – I didn't say nothing!'

Then he took James in and kept him for hundreds of hours.

James came out finally, looking white and sick, and all he'd say was that he wouldn't answer any more questions. Then Our Ma was called back in again, and James was taken into a different room, and I was left on my own.

It felt different, being on my own.

I soon got fed up of waiting. I wanted to go home.

I was hungry.

But I couldn't go home on my own – I wasn't even sure of the way. So I sat on this big wooden chair, drumming my heels against its legs. And after hundreds of hours this big woman comes out with a face like sour milk and says, 'You'd better come with me.'

Well I wasn't having that – I gave her the slip right away. I set off running down the stairs, but then I was pulled up, sharpish, for part way down the stairs there was a big window and through it I could see James and Our Ma being taken away!

I ran right up to the window and banged on it with the flat of my hands shouting, *Ma! Ma!* But it was like one of those dreams where no one can hear you – neither James nor Ma even looked up! And then Master Nowell appeared.

'Where are you taking them?' I cried, 'What's happening?'

But he just came right up to me and put his hands on my head and said, 'Gentle Jesus, meek and mild, help me save this little child.' Then he said to Sour-face, 'Take her to the Keeper's Lodge.'

'Where?' I said, and, 'I'm not going!' But Sour-face had caught up with me by this time, and she just kind of gathered up my hand and pulled me along.

On My Own

A New House

I was taken to this house on Master Nowell's land. And a woman in a long blue gown came out smiling. I didn't know who she was but she was nicer than Sour-face – pink cheeks and two shining wings of hair. I stood in a square hall and there was something rough under my feet, like new-cut grass only less prickly, and a big window with coloured glass.

Everybody had windows in their houses!

Sour-face left, but I had to stay.

I wasn't happy about that.

'Where's me Ma?' I said, and I couldn't say more because I felt like crying. But the woman knelt in front of me and I could see how shiny the hair was on either side of her parting – like polished wood, only soft – and before I could stop myself I reached out and touched one of them shiny wings of hair.

She didn't shout or slap me. She asked me if I'd like my hair done the same way. I just stared at her, gormless-like.

Then she took hold of my hand that had touched her, and all my skin jumped, but she only turned it one way then another, looking at the cuts and hard patches and dirt under the fingernails. Then she said I'd have to have a bath.

Well!

I'd never had one of them before.

I had to sit in a tub with no clothes on while water was poured over me! And when I squawked someone scrubbed my face with a rough cloth and I got this bitter taste in my mouth.

Least said about that the better.

Then I was dried off and given a whole different set of clothes – I don't know what'd happened to mine. There was a blue dress like the Lady's, but with little ribbons and bows down the front, and there were stockings and shoes!

I'd never worn shoes before.

But before I could put them on, one of the maids started going through my hair with something she called a *comb*.

It felt like she was trying to murder me – or at least pull my scalp off. I yelled as loud as I could and tried to climb off the chair, but she just kept hauling me back and holding me down with her great red hands.

She had arms like a woodcutter.

I wasn't crying, but her pulling my hair made my eyes water.

I didn't understand what she was trying to do.

When I tried to climb off again she pulled my hair

even harder and said she'd give me a thick ear if I didn't behave.

Now *that* I understood.

I decided I didn't like this place and I was going to run away. Only it was a bit difficult to run away with no clothes on, so I had to wait until I was dressed.

At last she finished, but then she started braiding my hair and pinning it up, and it took hundreds of hours.

Then I had to get dressed, only I didn't know how. So the maid tugged and pulled me into the clothes with this grim expression on her face as though she'd really have liked to chop me up!

Hatchet-face I called her.

And getting dressed took hours, too, because some things were too big and others too small, but she just kept on pushing and pulling me about, grimmer than ever, until the Lady came back. And then she stood me up to be looked at, and the Lady gave this little cry, so I wondered what I'd done.

'Now you look just like me!' she said.

I thought her eyesight must be going, but she nodded at the maid who wheeled this big thing round, like a copper plate in a wooden frame, and told me to look at myself.

Well, I looked, but I couldn't see me – just this little figure like a ghost girl, in a long blue dress – hair all parted and taken up just like the Lady's.

I put my hand out, but all that happened was my fingers touched the cold metal and made a mark. And the Lady laughed, a little silvery laugh, and stood behind me with her hands on my shoulders so that I could see her in the big plate too. And finally I realised it was me – me and her, like looking at my reflection in the well.

She said I'd got pretty hair.

No one had ever said that before.

I wanted to stick my tongue out at both of us, but I didn't. The Lady laughed again and said we were going to have such fun together – she'd never had a little girl before.

All the time I had the feeling that she wasn't really talking to me, but to the little doll-girl in the shiny plate.

She told me her name was Lady Ellen, but I could call her Mama, if I liked.

I didn't like!

When I just kept glaring and squinting at us both, she said, 'Don't you like the way you look?'

But I didn't know if I liked it or not. It didn't even look like me.

Of course, I know better than that now. I know that the long plate thing is called a *mirror*, and the lady would spend hours in front of it getting dressed. She couldn't even dress herself – she had two maids doing it for her. I know that the rough stuff under my feet was called *carpets*, and I learned, after a bit of effort, how to walk in shoes.

It wasn't easy. They seemed to want to walk a different way from my feet. Getting downstairs was downright dangerous!

The Lady had the mirror taken away and she inspected my fingers, which were a bit cleaner after my bath, and then she asked if I was hungry.

I was always hungry!

So I had to follow her downstairs in my new shoes, which was hard, but I could smell the food already, and that kept me going. I hobbled after her into a room where there was an enormous table and more food than I'd ever seen before in my life!

Great plates of meat swimming in gravy, and dried

fruit and different kinds of bread, and sauces and little cakes and soup and what looked like porridge.

I just stood there with my mouth open, then when I was told to sit down, I fell on the meat with my fingers and got the gravy all over my dress and there were cries of horror all round.

So that's another thing I had to learn – how to eat.

Seemed like rich folk just made everything as hard as they could.

But the meat was so tender, and the cakes were so sweet, I thought maybe I'd died and gone to heaven. And then I thought, maybe I wouldn't mind dying if it was like this!

After I'd eaten and eaten until my stomach felt like it was going to burst, I was taken up to my bedroom.

One bedroom, just for me, with a great big bed in it!

At home I slept on some straw in sacking, with Our Alizon's cold feet, not a real bed with a mattress and sheets.

Getting into this bed was a right palaver. I had to take my clothes off again, when it had taken so long to get them on, and then I had to put another set of clothes on, and have my hair unbraided, and *then* I had to kneel down and say a prayer.

I didn't know any, of course, or none that the Lady would've liked. Granny taught us a couple, but they were to do with witching. I didn't think it'd be a good idea to say them there, so I repeated after the Lady,

> *Matthew, Mark, Luke and John,*
> *Bless the bed that I lie on.*
> *Four corners to my bed,*
> *Four angels round my head;*
> *One to watch and one to pray,*
> *And two to bear my soul away.*

Which is downright creepy, if you ask me. Who wants four angels looming over them while they're asleep, waiting to take their soul off? So I said the words with one eye open, watching out for them angels, and with my fingers secretly crossed.

Then I had to get into the bed. I stood there at first, feeling doubtful, then I climbed in and it felt like it might swallow me whole! Like I might sink right down into it and never come up. Or that I'd slip about in the silky sheets till I rolled right out of it again.

How did rich people manage, with all this dressing and undressing and these slippery beds?

The Lady tucked me in so I couldn't fall out, and then she bent down and gave me this little kiss on the forehead and told me to sleep well.

A little kiss – like a moth brushing its wings on your skin!

No one had *ever* done that before!

She went out of the room then, and as soon as she'd gone I realised I hadn't asked about Our Ma. All my thoughts had been driven right out of my head.

I didn't know what to do, so I just lay there. I kept my head out of the bedclothes and gripped them tightly, so I didn't fall out and I kept my eyes wide open, staring into the shadows in case any angels came. I didn't want them taking my soul off.

No fear!

My Dream

Now even though I kept my eyes open, I must've fallen asleep, because I had this long, horrible dream.

I was back at Our House, looking for Our Ma, Our Alizon and Our James, but I couldn't find them anywhere.

I went round one corner then another, into a passageway, up and down some stairs.

Now, as you know, Malkin Tower didn't have any

passageways. Or stairs – it was just one room. But this was the dream.

Everything was cold and dark and deserted, but when I turned back the way I came, there was Our Granny, stirring her pot over the fire.

'Where is everyone?' I asked her, but she didn't look up.

'No one lives here anymore,' she said.

I turned round then, and there was the stairway again, big wooden stairs curving round, like in the Lady's house.

And at the top of them was the Lady, holding four great hounds on a leash.

I didn't have to look twice to know that they were Our Demons – Dandy, Ball and Tibb, and Our Alizon's that had no name. Their eyes glowed and their tails flicked like cats' tails do when they're angry. Tibb had this look on his face, like a cat that had been scalded.

'Where's Our Ma?' I cried, but the Lady said nothing, she just stared down at me. And when I turned back to Granny there was no one there – just ashes in an empty hearth.

That's when I woke up, heart banging.

I didn't know where I was at first. But as I lay there, wondering, Hatchet-face came to get me dressed and take me down for breakfast.

Breakfast!

Platefuls of steaming cakes and ham!

I forgot all about the dream.

The Lady was there, but she wasn't talking. When I tried to ask her about Our Ma, Hatchet-face shushed me up. The Lady kept her eyes closed, like she was praying, and picked away at her food, while I ate three platefuls of cakes and ham.

I thought she must've got drunk the night before, and was feeling a bit poorly.

Then I thought, *maybe she's got her own demons*. I tried to see them, but I couldn't.

I wished I was better at seeing demons. Or that Granny had taught me how to summon them. I'd have called them all up and we could've flown out of the window together!

I could just see the look on their faces – Hatchet-face and the Lady's – if we'd done that!

But it was no good. I couldn't summon them. I'd never learned how.

After breakfast Hatchet-face appeared with a blue cloak for me and a hat, and some wooden shoes that she slid over the shoes I already had on.

As if walking wasn't hard enough!

I clumped outside after her somehow though, and there was a carriage waiting – a big shiny carriage like the one I always thought my dad would come in! Just for a moment I thought it must be him, and my heart skipped, but then I saw who was driving it and he was old and fat, and he didn't have a crown, so I knew it couldn't be my dad.

Then I thought that maybe they were going to take me to Our Ma.

But they didn't take me to Our Ma, or Our Alizon or Our Granny. They took me back to him. Roger Nowell. The man with all the questions.

Well, I had some questions for him.

'Where's my Ma?' I asked, soon as I saw him. Of course he didn't answer.

'How do you like your new home?' he said. And I was about to ask when I could go back to my old one, but he said, 'Are they taking good care of you?'

'Yes,' I said, 'but – '

'Good,' he said. 'Have you eaten well?'

And he went on like this, asking all the questions, so I had to answer him and he didn't have to answer me. Then he said, 'Come and stand here, by my knee,' but I didn't move.

In my mind, whenever I think about that day, I'm standing there not moving, not saying anything. But I must've moved sometime, because I can also see myself standing by his knee. I remember the dark velvet of his breeches, his lacy collar, and the whites of his eyes. He had pale blue eyes, with little crescent moons of white under them, and the white bits were shot through with little red lines.

He could look at you for hundreds of hours without blinking.

Seems like there were two Jennets in that room, the one who stood still, saying nothing, and the one who went right up to him and told him everything he wanted to know.

Things I Told Him and Things He Told Me

First thing I remember him asking is, 'What about church, child?'

What about it? I didn't say.

'Do you go to church?'

Not if I can help it, I thought.

Then he said, 'Everyone has to go to church, by order of the king. Do you not like to go to church?'

I didn't say anything to that. Seemed like a trap to me.

When I didn't answer he asked me if I'd like something to eat. And even though I'd eaten three platefuls of breakfast I was still hungry. I had years of being hungry to make up for!

So he rang a little bell and a servant appeared and Master Nowell ordered some *refreshments,* and the servant disappeared again.

Good trick, that.

I wondered what'd happen if I rang a bell at home.

I'd probably have got a thick ear.

But there, in no time at all, the servant came back with a tray full of little cakes, all covered in sugar like they'd been dusted with snow. And he put the tray down in front of me!

I looked at Master Nowell with my mouth open and he nodded at me to show I could go ahead. I looked at him again – didn't *he* want some? – and he gave a little shake of his head.

So they were all for me!

Well, there was no point wasting time – I tucked in straight away.

They were quite small, the cakes, not quite small enough to fit in my mouth at one go, but if I stretched my mouth a bit sideways I could do it, even though I got sugar all down my chin and the front of my dress.

They tasted –

A bit funny actually. Sweet at first, where the sugar was, then not sweet at all. They stuck to the roof of my mouth and then melted away.

After I'd eaten a few I got a clagged up feeling as though my teeth might be stuck, and I had to push hard with my tongue to get my mouth moving again.

Luckily, he didn't ask me many questions while I was eating the cakes. Not at first, anyhow. He started telling me about the king, who was a Very Good King, and determined to rid the country of Heretics and Agents of Evil.

I must have looked blank, like my head had gone empty, because he asked me if I knew who the king was.

I could only think about my father.

But Master Nowell said that there was a king, not just of Pendle Forest, but of all England (wherever that is) and Scotland too (never heard of it). He was King James I of England and VI of Scotland.

I smirked a bit then at the thought of Our James being king.

'A King,' Master Nowell went on, speaking slow and heavy, 'Is like a father to his people.'

Like my father, I thought.

He said a lot more, about how this king had sent soldiers out to all parts of the country to look for witches. And he'd written a whole book called *Daemonologie* to help his men find demons.

I smirked a bit more at that. He didn't need to send out all his men – he could've just asked me! We had lots of demons!

I thought it was probably best not to say that, though.

Master Nowell had been told by this king to make a list of all the people who didn't go to church every Sunday.

That'll be a long list, I thought. I didn't know anyone who went every Sunday. Granny hadn't been for years!

Next he asked me if I knew any prayers.

I hung my head a bit and mumbled the one the Lady had taught me the night before.

'That's very good,' he said. 'Do you know any others?'

I hung my head some more. But he waited. He had this way of waiting that drew words out of you. Like he was in no hurry at all, he could sit there like Our Hill, not moving, for the rest of your life.

The only other prayers I knew were Granny's charms.

In the end I whispered them to him, and he told me to speak up.

I said he were a bit deaf.

So I started again.

Upon Good Friday I will fast while I may
Until I hear them knell
Our Lord's own bell
Open, open heaven door keys,
Steck, steck hell door – !

'Hush child!' he cried, and when I looked up he'd clamped his hands over his ears. 'That's no prayer,' he said, and, 'Such words are not for you.'

Well, he asked!

Then he said, 'Can you say them again?'

Make your mind up, I thought, but he just waited. So I did say them out loud again, in full. And this time he wrote my words down!

Real writing, with a feather and ink!

I wished I could read what he wrote – or even better – that I could write for myself. You never know what someone else is writing about you.

When he finished he looked at me over the top of two

shiny bits of glass on his nose, and asked me, 'What do you know about witchcraft?'

Well, I could've said, *not a lot*, being as I'm no good at it, and try though I might none of my spells ever work. Or I could've said *lots*, being as I was born into it, and my whole family were witches.

While I was still thinking about what to say, he asked me another question. 'Are you aware that all witchcraft is an evil thing, of the Devil, and abhorrent to the Lord?'

Well, there were two ways of looking at that one as well. One was his – which was to say that it was all bad and devilish. And the other was that it was what poor folk like us had always done. It was just the way things were. As for it being an *evil* thing – that I wasn't sure about. My Granny had made lots of people well.

When I didn't answer that one, he tried a different tack.

Was I aware that certain people had accused my family of witchcraft?

That one was easy. I nodded my head hard and managed to swallow the rest of the cake in my mouth.

'What do you make of that?' he asked. 'The fact that people think your family are witches?'

'Well, they *are* witches,' I told him, and for the first

time he looked surprised.

'What do you mean by that?' he said, but I couldn't think how to say it any plainer.

'*All* witches?' he said and I just nodded at him. Of course they were. That's what caused all the trouble. Then he asked me what I thought it meant – how did I know they were witches, which seemed like a soft question to me, so I said nothing and he asked me, 'What do they do, as witches?'

And I found myself telling him then, about Our Granny who was the first one and how she made Our Ma a witch, and then Our Alizon and Our James, but not me, never me. She said I was too young, but James said it was because I had a different father –

I started feeling angry then, with the same old anger, that I was the one treated different. And that, for all their demons and powers, none of them had ever done anything good. Like get us a better place to live or a house like Master Nowell's or the Lady's where we could eat food all day off a big gold plate.

I got more and more annoyed, telling him stuff, but then Master Nowell interrupted me.

'Speak more clearly, child,' he said.

What did he mean? *He* was the one that spoke funny, like rich folk spoke. But I had to say it all over again, and even then he didn't understand some of my words. So in the end he asked me a different question.

'What can you tell me about your father, child?' he said.

My father?

I didn't know how to answer that one. It didn't seem right to say that I thought he might be the king. Or *a* king. Somehow, it didn't seem likely anymore.

I shook my head.

And that's when he told me I've got a Father in Heaven, which was news to me. He was looking out for me, this Father, because He loved me, and He thought I was something special.

No one told me that's where my dad was!

This Father was King of Heaven, and Heaven was His House, he said. A place of wonder and light, where we'd all stand before God, our Heavenly Father.

Thought he were *my* heavenly father.

Then he asked if I knew what heaven was like.

I'd just started another cake, but I looked up at him with my mouth half full and said, 'Is it like this?'

'No, no, child,' he said, half shocked, half laughing. But I could tell he was a little bit pleased at the thought of his house being like heaven. Which would make him like God, I suppose.

He told me a bit about heaven, then, about how we wouldn't have to do much there, we wouldn't have to forage or beg for food. We'd just stand round God and sing his praises.

Which'd be all right, I suppose, but I thought my heaven'd be a big square room like Master Nowell's, with windows that had real glass in them, and carpets on the floor and polished wood, and servants bringing you as much as you could eat every day!

Then he moved on to Hell, which, as everyone knows, is nowhere near as nice. Way he talked about it though, it was quite bloodcurdling – all about being roasted in a fire till your eyeballs pop, for all eternity! Which is a long time to keep a fire going.

Where would they get all that wood, for the fires?

He kept on talking while I thought about the last cakes and whether it'd look too greedy if I ate them all. I made a start, anyway, in spite of the stomach ache I was starting to get, but then I could feel him looming over me and when I looked up those two pale eyes were looking right down into mine.

And suddenly I couldn't even chew.

'You can save them, Jennet,' he said in a low voice, almost whispering. 'You can save their souls.'

Then he sat back down in his chair, still looking at me. He rested his elbows on the chair arms and pressed his fingertips together and gazed at me until I lost my appetite, and then he asked, 'Wouldn't you like to save your family, Jennet?'

Words

I've thought about it a lot since, and all I can think is, there's more than one meaning to certain words, like *save*, and *truth*. There's what he meant, and there's what I meant.

Same as, there's more than one word for different things. There was my word, and there was his.

Like, when I looked out of the window and said, 'It's hossin' it down.'

And he stopped writing and gave me that look, over them two bits of glass, and said, 'Do you mean it's raining hard?'

I gave him a look of my own. *Everyone* knows what hossin' it down means.

When I didn't answer he said he would have to teach me to speak the King's English. I didn't know the king *had* an

English. How could I learn to speak like the king? But Master Nowell said the truth could only be spoken in the King's English.

He said that as long as I told the truth I could save my family and we would all stand before my Father in Heaven. I could see myself introducing Our Alizon and Our James to him. Because he'd be *my* father – not theirs!

It sounds daft now, so daft I can hardly believe it, but I believed it then, and I believed him when he said that as long as I listened to him and did as he said, everything'd be fine.

Or at least, I believed what I wanted to believe. Now I know that's not exactly the same thing. But I didn't know that then.

There wasn't just one of these meetings – there were hundreds of them! Or at least a lot more.

They all started the same way, with cakes. First the cakes, then the questions. When he liked my answers he'd laugh and send for more cakes, and call me his good little girl.

Well I wasn't his girl. But after I'd seen him any number of times something odd started to happen. I started to know what to say, how to please him – how to get them cakes.

But it wasn't just about the cakes. When I said the right thing his face lit up – it was like standing in the warm glow of the sun after a cold dark winter. And soon I knew exactly how to make that sun shine.

I didn't always want to, of course. Sometimes I just wasn't in the mood. Sometimes I took against him and his fancy words – then I'd get it wrong deliberately or pretend I'd forgot, or just stand there with a stupid expression on my face like it was all too much and he was just too clever for me. The only thing I'd say was 'Can I go home now?' I wondered if I could make him lose his temper just for fun.

But he didn't. Only once did I see him get annoyed, and that was when I said that his prayers were the same as charms, sort of, because they were, but I saw his face change and I thought I was for it. But he only turned away, and I heard him muttering, *no better than a savage*, and that annoyed *me* a bit, because he seemed to think we were like animals. By the time he turned round again I had the stupid expression back on my face and he sighed, and I could see him making himself go over the same old ground again.

I'd never met anyone like him before, big and

important-looking and patient as Our Hill. He could've sat there with me all day, going over what I said, making me repeat stuff after him, because rich folk have got nothing else to do.

I had to wait too, of course, while he wrote stuff down. I was nowhere near as good at it. I fidgeted and shuffled and dropped things. Or kicked the legs of the chair and wondered when I could go home.

I missed Malkin Tower. Yes! Even the bare dirty floor and the old bed of sacking that ran with mice and lice! Even the leaking roof! Sounds daft to say it, but I'd have given it all up if I could have gone home with Our Ma and Our Granny and Our Alizon, and even Our James.

I was even missing James by then!

Course I didn't say any of that to Master Nowell. By that time I'd got it all worked out – that the only way to get back with my family was to do everything just the way he wanted, say all the right words in the right way, and get us all back home where we belonged so that we could get on with our lives.

That's what I thought about while he was writing. But I couldn't help fidgeting and messing about. Then one day Master Nowell stopped writing and looked at me over the top of them little bits of glass.

I thought he was going to tell me off, but instead he said, 'Do you think you would be able to repeat these words in court?'

I didn't know what *court* was – he had to explain that one to me.

He told me that the court was in the castle – like where the king lived, only instead of the king there was a judge, and a jury – big important men, who'd listen to everything I'd say and write it down.

I was an Important Witness, he said. And an Agent of the Lord.

Me!

So then we had to practise what I had to say in court and we had to change some of what I said into Master Nowell's words – the Lord's words he called them, we were practising the Lord's words, in the King's English.

I couldn't say *Our Ma* in court. I had to say *My mother*, even though it meant the same thing. And I couldn't say *clemmed*, I had to say hungry, and not *warridn*, but cursed. And when I said Our Granny had fixed someone's arm with a *spelk*, meaning splinter of wood, he said I had to say *spell*.

The more it went on, the better I got at it, and the more I felt like a new Jennet standing there in her new dress and new shoes, saying important words – not the old Jennet in her scruffy rags, that no one ever listened to. I'd left her back in Malkin Tower.

Soon I was word perfect and he got more and more pleased with me and with everything I said, until one day he said I was ready.

I didn't say, r*eady for what?* But I soon found out.

I was ready to say all them words before a judge, in court.

Where everyone'd be listening – to me!

Court

he First Day

Getting me ready for court took hundreds of hours. I had to have another bath! And the Lady combed my hair herself – it wasn't so tangled this time, so I didn't want to scream and bite her. She braided it again, threading ribbons through it this time, and pinned it up. Then we smiled at one another in the mirror.

'You look like God's little angel,' she said, and I thought, *Agent. I'm an Agent of the Lord*. But I didn't say it.

And then Sour-face came, to take me off.

I didn't want to go with her. 'Aren't you coming?' I asked the Lady, but she only said she'd be waiting for me when I got back. Then Sour-face took me outside where a carriage was waiting to take us all the way to the castle.

I'd never been to a castle before! We rode all the way there in the carriage, me and Sour-face with other people as well. No one said anything, except for me. I said things like, 'Will the king be in?' But no one answered. No one spoke to me at all, except to tell me off when I poked my head out of the carriage window to get a better look.

The castle was bigger than anything I'd ever seen – apart from Our Hill. It was like Our Hill, only with walls.

As we got closer I could see round towers on either

side of huge gates. We were stopped at the gates by men with pikes, and I poked my head back inside quick. Then we rode in through the gates and it was like riding into the heart of Our Hill!

I felt a bit sick, actually. I was thinking, *what if it all falls down? What happens if it all comes tumbling down on us?*

Then we had to get out of the carriage and walk across a great stone courtyard, my wooden shoes went clop, clop, clop all the way.

We went up some steps, and then some more steps, and I could just see a great long hall. But I was taken into a little room, to one side of it, and told to wait until I was called.

Then I really felt sick!

And I had to wait for hundreds of hours. All that time I didn't know what was happening, so I looked down at my dress and my shoes and remembered that I was an Important Witness and an Agent of the Lord.

Then someone called my name.

JENNET DEVICE

Not just once, but lots of times:

JENNET DEVICE, JENNET DEVICE, JENNET DEVICE.

I looked up at Sour-face and she gave me a nod. It was

my turn at last.

Then she prodded me a bit when I didn't move, and I had to follow this man into the courtroom.

When I went into that big room I couldn't see Our Ma at first for all the fine folk. There were hundreds of eyes watching me. I worked out who the judge was, in his big seat, even though he didn't have a crown. There was no sign of the king, though, and I still couldn't see Our Ma. Then when I did see her I hardly recognised her – she was so thin and ragged-looking and yellowish. But she recognised me, all right. Soon as her bad eye landed on me she gave an awful screech and started calling out all the worst names she could think of, till even the judge turned blue. She said I was no child of hers, and she told me exactly what she'd do if she got hold of me.

And do you know what?

Straight away I changed. I wasn't Jennet Device, Master Nowell's good and clever little girl in a brand new frock and shoes. I was Skinny Jen the Malkin Child, who couldn't get anything right, and couldn't even do spells.

The change happened so fast I felt all trembly and sick inside. I looked round for Master Nowell and burst into tears.

Judge rapped on the table and told Our Ma to 'Be Quiet!' in a thundery sort of voice, but she just kept right on screeching.

I remembered that I had to call the judge m'lord.

'Please sir – m'lordship – I can't say it – I can't say nothing while she's here. Take her away!' I cried, but what I really meant was, take me away – the me I couldn't bear to look at – the scruffy little beggar girl.

And the judge shook his big head and ordered the guards to take Our Ma away.

I could still hear her screeching even after she left the room. Then all at once it went quiet, and I felt a bit better. Like she'd put a spell on me, just being there. But now I could stand up and my knees weren't knocking quite so much. And I could see Master Nowell nodding at me in an encouraging kind of way, and all them words we'd practised came back to me. So I took a deep breath and started:

My mother is a witch and this I know to be true, for I have seen her spirit come to her many times in the shape of a brown dog called Ball…

On and on I went, about how she'd been a witch three or four years, and how she told Ball to help her kill John and James Robinson of Barley, and Henry Mitton of Roughlee.

It was easy.

And when I'd finished you could've heard a pin drop in that room. All them fine gentlemen staring at me like I'd just said the most important thing in the world! And Master Nowell – he looked so proud!

No one had ever looked at me like that before.

And then they brought Our Ma back into court.

I ducked back down into my seat, quick.

She was still ranting and raving, so the judge had to shout at her again. She was that dirty and awful and full of venom – I felt – not just scared of her this time, but *ashamed* – ashamed she were my Ma.

I didn't ever want to be like that. Like her.

Everything she'd said in her confession and everything I'd said and other people had said was read out to her, and she kind of collapsed, fell forward with her face hidden by her dirty yellow fingers.

'Have mercy on me!' she cried.

My heart was wrung then, I can't say it wasn't. My lips moved and I whispered, *Ma*.

But I had to remind myself that it was for her

own good in the long run – she had to stop doing that old witchcraft that brought us nothing but trouble.

Next to be brought up was Our James. If anything he looked even worse – one side of his face all battered and blue. And much thinner and dirtier than when I saw him last – clothes hanging off him in tatters.

All the charges were read out against him – about how he'd put curses on Mistress Towneley who'd accused him of stealing turf, and then on Master John Duckworth who said he'd give him a shirt, but didn't, and then I was called up again.

You should've seen James's face when I walked out in my new clothes and shoes (I was getting the hang of them shoes by then). Looked like he didn't know who I was, then when he did he was dumbstruck.

And I piped up clearly and said, 'Yes – he's been a witch about three years now, and he's got a demon that comes to him in the form of a black dog called Dandy. And I was with him when he told it to harm Mistress Towneley!'

This time I wasn't scared at all. I looked round at the court and I could see they were all impressed. One man wrote down everything I said!

And James couldn't deny it – he didn't even try.

Then there were more charges read out against

him, about John Hargraves of Goldshawbooth, and Blaize Hargreives of Higham.

And I stood up and said, 'Yes, he definitely did it – and he called up his demon, Dandy to help.'

Judge asked me to say the two charms that James used, and I said them straight out, word perfect! Even the one in a funny language, *crucifixus hoc signam…* that was to get drink. And the other was the one I told Master Nowell, to cure someone who's bewitched, which I spoke out loud and clear.

> *Open, open heaven door keys!*
> *Steck, steck hell door!*

I always liked that bit. But as a charm it were no good, I can tell you that much. It never worked.

Our James went a funny colour though – kind of green. And when the judge asked him if it was true he just kind of mumbled, *yes*.

And that was more or less it for that day.

Master Nowell came to tell me how well I'd done and how clever I was, and that night we stayed at an inn. I'd never stayed at an inn before. I got to eat and drink all I could.

But part way through I started thinking about what they were eating – Our Ma and Our Alizon and Our James, and suddenly the food didn't taste so good any more.

I wished the trial was over, and we could all go home.

I had to share a room with Sour-face, and she snored like a bear, so I didn't sleep much at all. I lay awake in the strange bed in the strange room, thinking about how the next day would be in court, and worrying about what I had to say. All the right words, in the King's English, just as he told me. For him – Master Nowell.

The Second Day

For breakfast there was porridge and bread, and then we set off again for the castle. This time I could see how gloomy it looked, like a big, gloomy prison. I had to wait in the little room again for hundreds of hours, because more people were on trial that day. Finally I was called in, and asked about the meeting at Malkin Tower. I had to stand up and say:

Upon Good Friday last there were about twenty persons,
but only two of them were men as I remember – at my
grandmother's house called Malkin Tower, at about
twelve o'clock.

I couldn't say *Our Granny,* same as I couldn't say *Our Ma.* I
had to say *my grandmother*, so the judge would know what I
meant.

I told him that they were all witches at the meeting
and that they had come to give a name to my sister's spirit or
demon, for it had no name yet. And I told him about all the
food – that we all had beef, bacon *and* roast mutton for our
dinners – and that I saw the sheep killed and roasted.

The judge asked me if I could name the witches there,
but I could only remember about six of them, and so he said,
'Would you recognise them if you saw them?'

And I said I would – I've got a good memory, me!

So he arranged it like this.

All the prisoners had to go into the upper hall, where
they were mixed up with other prisoners and with complete
strangers. And they had to stand in a line. And then I was
taken in and told to pick out the ones who were at Malkin
Tower that day.

Straight away I walked up to Alice Nutter and took

her by the hand. I could even say who she sat next to and what she'd said!

Then the judge said, 'Was Joan-a-Style at the meeting?'

Trying to trick me, you see, with a made up name. But I didn't fall for it – I said very clearly that there was no such woman there, nor did I know that name. And I went straight up to the next witch – this being Katherine Hewitt, or *Mould-Heels* as everyone called her – and I took her by the hand as well.

Then that judge, still trying to catch me out, asked if Joan-a-Down was there – another made up name – so I said again that there was no such woman there, and I'd never heard of her.

That shut him up.

I went on like this, taking Jane Bulcocke by the hand and John Bulcocke, who helped roast the sheep, until everyone was picked out. And then I remembered something. I turned to the judge and said,

'There's one woman who's not here.'

He looked surprised at this, as well he might, for it proved I wasn't making it up. The woman I was talking about was Jennet Preston, and I found out later that she'd been taken away and tried at York.

On my way back to my seat I saw Sour-face talking to Master Nowell, and nodding, then she made her way back to me.

'Come child,' she said. 'Your work here is done.'

Well I wasn't happy about that. That meant I wouldn't get to see the rest of the prisoners being tried. And I'd not seen Our Alizon yet!

How did Sour-face know I wouldn't be needed again?

I was an Important Witness, me!

But I wasn't supposed to talk out of turn in court, so I couldn't argue with her, and anyway, she wouldn't have stood for any arguments. She just tucked my hand into hers like before, and off we went.

On the way out it seemed to me like everyone was looking at me funny, but I didn't know why.

All this being clever was giving me a headache!

Afterwards

our-face

On my way out I saw Master Nowell talking to two men. I broke away from Sour-face and ran up to him crying, 'Master Nowell, Sir, Master Nowell, how did I do?'

He looked at me for a moment and then – he went on talking!

So I went right up to him and tugged at his sleeve. Then he looked, not at me, but at Sour-face, who was hurrying up behind.

'See to it that she has a good meal,' he said, still not looking at me. And then he said something else, about taking me back to the Lady, but I wasn't listening.

Why wouldn't he look at me?

I tugged at his sleeve again, but Sour-face pulled me away. Then at last he did look – but such a look! I hope no one ever gives me a look like that again!

There was pity in it, and bad feeling, and something else – sort of sly.

But more than anything it was as though he wished he never had to look at me again.

He said something like, 'You'll be well taken care of, child, never fear,' and gave a little laugh that wasn't really a laugh, and then he turned back to his friends.

They were both staring at me.

All the words I had to say just dried up and stuck in my throat.

I let myself be pulled away by Sour-face, back to the carriage, and still I couldn't say anything. I couldn't say, 'Why did they look at me like that?' because she'd only say, 'Like what?' or pretend she hadn't seen.

But as the carriage rolled away I thought, *what about being an Agent of the Lord and Master Nowell's good, clever little girl? What about saving my family and seeing my Father in Heaven?*

I'd had enough of all this by then. I just wished things would get back to the way they were. I didn't want to go back to the Lady's to be fussed over and have ribbons put in my hair and such – I didn't even want to eat cake. I wanted to go back to Malkin Tower, with Our Granny and Our Ma and Our Alizon and even Our James. I hoped that old judge wouldn't keep them too long in prison.

I just wanted things to get back to normal.

But they didn't get normal – they got worse.

We went back to the Lady's house, but the Lady wasn't there, not at first, and Sour-face had a long talk to Hatchet-face, who glanced over at me, very stern and grim. I didn't say anything, I didn't move or speak, and when they'd finished talking I followed Hatchet-face, meek as you like up the stairs.

Where I was told to get myself ready for bed.

'What about tea?' I asked then, for Master Nowell had told Sour-face to see to it I had a good meal. But Hatchet-face gave me a look that was savage, even for her.

'If you think the cook's going to trouble herself for the likes of you –' she hissed. That was all she said, but I knew something had changed – something had gone wrong, but I didn't know what.

When she'd gone I got undressed like she said, and climbed into that big cold bed with the slippery sheets, and lay very still under the covers in that dark room, as if I could make myself much smaller than I already was. Smaller and smaller, until I was hardly there at all.

I must've fallen asleep eventually, despite being hungry, but all night long I could hear Ma's voice chanting this song that she used to sing to me when I was really small:

> *There was a little girl,*
> *And her name was Jen,*
> *She wasn't much bigger*
> *Than a speckled hen*
> *She wasn't much louder*
> *Than a sparrow's tweet,*

But she liked to drink and she liked to eat,
And she grew up big and noisy!

atchet-face

The next morning I woke up and I didn't know where I was. But I knew I was hungry. No one came to me in my room, so I got myself dressed as best as I could, and went downstairs.

I could hear voices from the kitchen so I went in there. There was a group of servants standing together, but they all stopped talking when they saw me. And they looked at me funny.

'What's going on?' I said, trying to smile. 'Where is everyone?'

Hatchet-face stepped out of the group, then she stood still, staring at me like the others. I caught one of them making the sign of the cross.

My legs felt funny and my mouth went dry.

'What is it?' I started to say, but it came out no bigger than a whisper. Then Hatchet-face walked towards me, and I tried not to flinch.

'Breakfast,' was all she said, and I followed her out of

the kitchen.

She left me sitting at the big table, looking at my face in the shiny wood, for hundreds of hours.

I just sat there, because I didn't know what else to do.

When she came back, I said, 'Where's the Lady?'

But she just carried on putting out a bowl and spoon. So I asked her again, a bit louder. And she stopped what she was doing and gave me the kind of look that'd crush a beetle.

'She'll be back,' she said. And she went out again, leaving me with a bowl of porridge. But I wasn't hungry anymore.

I ate it anyway, and went back up to my room, away from all the funny looks and whispering. I watched out of the window for a sign of Master Nowell or the Lady.

It was a long time before the carriage arrived. I saw it pull to a halt and the driver helped the Lady down.

She was wearing a green silk dress and a cloak.

Something stopped me from running downstairs.

I saw her talking to Hatchet-face, then she came in.

At last I went down the stairs really quietly, but they heard me anyway and looked up. Hatchet-face looked pleased with herself, yet still as though she had something nasty under her nose. But the Lady – the Lady looked as if she'd seen a ghost. As if she didn't know who I was anymore.

She pressed a piece of lace to her mouth, then said something like, 'Not now – I must rest.' And she walked off without speaking to me.

By this time I'd had enough.

I came down the rest of the stairs until I was standing three from the bottom, and I could more or less look Hatchet-face straight in the eye.

'I want to go home,' I said.

There was that look again, like she was about to spit out a frog.

Our James did that once.

She pursed her mouth right up and her eyes almost disappeared.

'You've got no home,' she said. 'Haven't you heard? They've hung all the witches up on the moor.'

The Worst Thing Ever

For a minute my lips wouldn't work. Then I said, 'What – what did you say?' And 'No.' And 'That's not right!'

She made a great show of looking at the clock.

'They've hung them,' she said. 'Your Ma and all the

rest of your family – and seven others too. Thanks to you.'

There was a roaring noise in my ears and everything turned upside down, and then the right way up again. I don't remember very clearly what happened next. But one thing I do remember.

The demons.

I could see them, clear as day.

Dandy, Ball, Tibb and the nameless one stood with me on the stair, all in the shape of hounds. They were with me when I leapt on her.

We went straight for her throat.

Hatchet-face fell back shrieking and everyone came running.

Someone said, 'It's the devil – the devil's got her!'

The Lady cried, 'Take her – take her away!'

Seemed like I wasn't her little doll-girl anymore.

It took three of them to prise me off Hatchet-face, my fingers from round her throat, her face all purple and goggle-eyed. Then two of them carried me upstairs, me kicking and biting all the way. They shut the door on me and I battered myself against it until I'd near enough knocked myself out.

Later, the doctor came, and the priest. One held a cross over me and the other made me drink something sweet and powerful that burned my throat.

After that I didn't remember much at all.

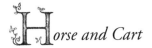

Horse and Cart

Glimpses and voices came and went in a big blur. I heard someone say that I couldn't stay at the Lady's anymore, but no one knew where to put me.

I didn't even care. Only person I wanted to see was Master Nowell, and they wouldn't let me see him.

He *told* me – he said if I told the truth just like he taught me, they'd all be saved!

Now I knew he'd told me a pile of big fat lies.

I stopped talking, now I knew all the trouble words could cause. Stopped eating too. I stayed in my room and different people came and went, talking over my head.

Then one day it seemed like someone had come to a decision, because a new maid, not Hatchet-face, appeared with some clothes.

'Get up and get dressed,' she said.

I didn't move.

She stripped the bedclothes back. 'None of your games,' she said. 'Get up!'

I was tired of lying there by that time, so I got up slowly and did as I was told. And then I followed her outside, where there was a horse and cart.

No one came to say goodbye, but I could feel them all looking from the windows. I didn't look back. I didn't even ask where we were going. I just sat in the front of that cart as it rocked and rumbled from side to side. The driver said nothing either. But everyone we passed stopped and stared.

I wouldn't look at them but in my mind I could feel them watching, and hear what they were thinking.

> *Jennet, Jennet, what have you done?*
> *Trial's over and you've had your fun.*
> *Sold your mother, your sister and your brother too –*
> *Watch out for the devil, he's coming for you!*

And all I could think was, *Shut up, you lot! Shut up – shut up!*

Mistress Alice

I was taken to this cottage on the far side of Pendle Hill. A woman lived there on her own. She had a broad, kind face.

Said her name was Mistress Alice. But that just reminded me of Alizon.

Horse and cart rolled away and she held out her hand.

I didn't say anything. I didn't care if I never spoke again.

But Mistress Alice didn't look at me like I was a freak or a monster. Nor did she fuss over me like I was a doll and call me her little girl. She didn't say much at all. She just got on with stuff and I had to help – milking the cow, collecting eggs, shelling peas. We went to church on Sundays.

I didn't want to at first, but we just slipped in at the back and no one stared.

It was all right, I suppose.

She taught me a lot of prayers and read to me sometimes. Apart from that, we didn't talk much. I didn't want to talk, and I didn't want to remember.

The house was nowhere near as big as the Lady's, or Master Nowell's, but it was better than Malkin Tower. There were two rooms and the roof didn't leak.

So it seemed I'd got myself that better life. Clean and safe. Plenty to eat. No one bossing me about. She never hit me, Mistress Alice.

And yet…

I still dreamed about them at night and expected them

to be there when I woke up. Sometimes I felt as though they were watching me while I did stuff, cleaning out the chickens, sweeping the yard, or I'd hear their voices,

Jennet, Jennet, what have you done?

But when I turned round, there was no one there.

And no demons, either – I looked. I don't know where they went. I hope they went to Master Nowell's, and got him by the throat.

Or maybe they were with Our Ma, and Our Alizon, and Our Granny and Our James, looking after them. Maybe Alizon would've given hers a name by now.

Anyway, there were no demons here, in this house. Only in my head.

One day, months and months after it all happened, I was sitting on a bench in the yard, peeling turnips with a knife. I cut into them with short, hard strokes and more and more of the turnip came away with the peel. Mistress Alice looked my

way.

She sat down next to me on the bench, I could feel the warmth of her through her dress.

'What is it, Jennet?' she said, and when I didn't answer she said, 'Have you remembered something?'

'No.' I said.

'Maybe you need to remember,' she said.

I turned to her then and gave her a long look.

'Remember what I did?' I said. Which was the first time either of us had ever mentioned it.

She didn't answer at first. Then she said, 'You can remember that you loved them.'

A big sore place opened up in me then, and I wanted to howl, but I didn't. I closed my eyes.

And there they all were – Our Granny, Our Ma, Our Alizon, Our James. All looking at me.

But this time I didn't look away. I looked right back at them, and it's as if I could see them clearly for the first time.

I could see how all their chanting and spelling never did them any good. None of their words had any real power.

No one listened to them – not really. No one listened to their side of the story. Same as no one listened to me.

If Roger Nowell had his way no one'd listen to anyone but him.

But everyone's got a story, and if they don't tell it, then other people'll tell it for them.

And maybe they'll end up hanged.

All those thoughts came to me then as I sat on the bench in that yard with my eyes closed. When I opened them I was looking at Our Hill, big and broad and peaceful, just like it always was, the very top of it hidden by cloud. And I knew then what I'd never known before.

There's only one way to make your words have power, and that's to tell your own story, in your own way.

That's why I'm telling it now.

To you.

Acknowledgements

The author would like to thank Robert Poole and Chris Goodier for being unfailingly helpful and generous, and Colin Penny for a fascinating tour of Lancaster Castle.

Find out more...

When Jennet Device gave evidence in court in 1612, one man was writing everything down. Thomas Potts was a clerk of the court and his account of the trial, *The Wonderfull Discoverie of Witches in the Countie of Lancaster*, is the only evidence that has survived. You can explore a modernised version of his account online at:

www.lancashirewitches.com

Stepping Stones Nigeria

The persecution of children and adults for alleged acts of witchcraft is not an issue that has been consigned to history – it is still damaging lives across the world today.

Stepping Stones Nigeria is a UK-based charity working to uphold the rights of children in the Niger Delta region in Africa, where there is a deeply held belief in child 'witches'. Stepping Stones Nigeria work with Nigerian partner organisations to protect these children and prevent modern-day witch hunts.

Visit their website to find out more about their vital work:

www.steppingstonesnigeria.org